For 'Flying Time' with Miles,
Chloe and Poppy – with my love

JANETTA OTTER-BARRY BOOKS

Text and illustrations copyright © Catherine Hyde 2016
The right of Catherine Hyde to be identified as the author and illustrator
of this work has been asserted by her in accordance with the
Copyright, Designs and Patents Act, 1988 (United Kingdom).

First published in Great Britain and in the USA in 2016 by
Frances Lincoln Children's Books,
74-77 White Lion Street, London N1 9PF
www.franceslincoln.com

A CIP catalogue record for this book is available from the British Library.

ISBN 978-1-84780-672-7

Illustrated with oil pastel and pencil

Printed in China

9 8 7 6 5 4 3 2 1

MIX
Paper from
responsible sources
FSC® C008047

The Star Tree

Catherine Hyde

Frances Lincoln
Children's Books

In the still, quiet room in the sleeping house,
the beautiful horse with a golden mane
shines in the moonlight.

Magical.

Waiting.

Ready.

Tick.
The house breathes in.
Tock.
The house breathes out.

It is midnight at Midsummer and Mia is awake.
The night-light has gone out
but the silvery moon shines in.
A soft breeze stirs the curtains.
Mia tiptoes towards the horse.
Outside, in the warm night,
an owl hoots.

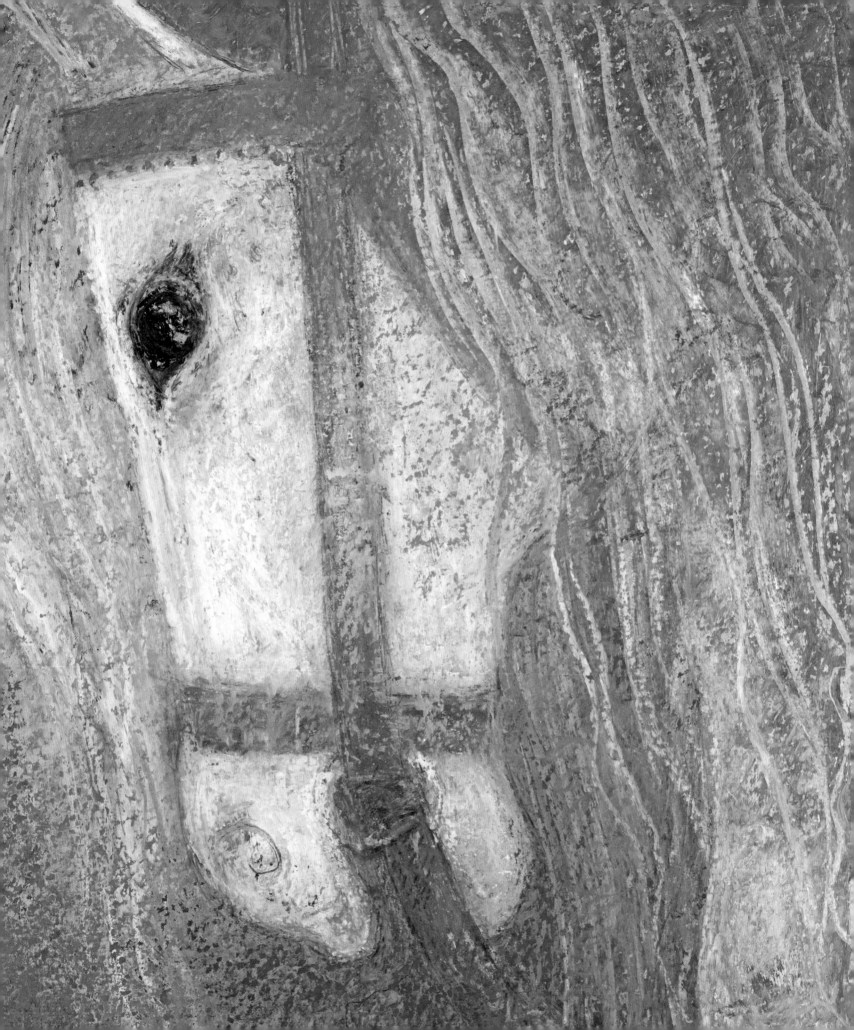

In the dreaming house,
   Mia climbs on the wonderful horse
      and rocks to and fro, to and fro,
   swinging high, swinging low
      as she wishes on the
   Midsummer Moon.

And as she wishes,
the Great White Owl
comes flying to the window
and sings...

"Climb onto my back,
Fly away with me,
Over the hills and
Down to the sea.

Sail in the boat with the Little Red Hare,
Over the ocean, over the waves,
Out to the island,
Out to the Bear.

Fly up to the planets,
Up through the stars,
This side is Venus,
That side is Mars.

Away to the north,
Away to the snow
Where the skies sing songs
And the Giant Stag goes.

Climb onto my back,
Ride away with me.
We are looking for the land
With a light in a tree."

Mia and the Owl glide silently
        into the velvet night.
                Under the big yellow moon
        they fly along the tops of the trees,
                away from the houses,
        away from the shops,
                away from the church
                        where the blunted weather vane
                                barely stirs.
                                Over the hills
                                        and down
                                                to the sea.

"Climb on board and sail away with me,
into the night and far out to sea,"
calls the Little Red Hare.

With the wind in her sails
the little boat goes up and then up,
up and then down,
over the ocean, over the waves,
out to the island, out to the Bear.

"Climb into my basket and fly away with me,"
smiles the Big White Bear.

"Higher and higher, up through the clouds,
up to the planets, up to the stars.
This side is Venus, that side is Mars.
Away to the north, away to the snow
where the sky sings songs
and the Giant Stag goes."

The Giant Stag cries,
"Climb onto my back,
ride away with me.
We must climb a high hill
to find the Star Tree."

Mia and the Giant Stag gallop

    up the icy path, through the fragrant trees,

past the prowling wolf

    and the mountain hare

      to the very top of the high hill....

The Star Tree shimmers and sparkles
in the glittering night.
And as the snow falls
and the stars bloom
and the sky shines,
Mia plucks
one
small
star
from the gleaming tree.

And as the snow falls and the sky sings,

    Mia holds her star and the Great White Goose

comes to take her home.

    Away they fly, down from the high hill of stars

        and the fragrant trees.

Back across the vast ocean and the Big White Bear's island.

Away from the boat and the Little Red Hare.
Homeward along the river's silver pathway.
Up and over the drowsy land, over the hills,
over the church with the blunted weather vane
that barely stirs in the still air.

Over the rooftops, over the gardens
and back in through the moonlit window.

In the still, quiet room in the sleeping house,
the beautiful horse with a golden mane
shines in the moonlight.
Magical.
Waiting.
Ready.

It is midnight at Midsummer.

    The night-light glimmers, star-like.

Mia is asleep.

Tick.

The house breathes in.

Tock.

The house breathes out.